The pencil

Beverley   Randell
Illustrated   by   Isabel   Lowe

"Where is my tail?"
said the dog.

"Here it is,"

said the pencil.

"Where is my ear?"
said the cat.

"Here it is,"

said the pencil.

"Where is my eye?"

said the cow.

"Here it is,"

said the pencil.

"Where is my leg?"
said the sheep.

"Here it is,"

said the pencil.

"Where is my nose?"
said the pig.

"Here it is,"

said the pencil.

"Where is my horn?"
said the goat.

"Here it is,"

said the pencil.

"Where are my wings?"
said the duck.

"Here they are,"

said the pencil.

16